Volcanic Rocks

Connor Dayton

PowerKiDS
press™
New York

Published in 2007 by The Rosen Publishing Group, Inc.
29 East 21st Street, New York, NY 10010

First Edition

Editor: Jennifer Way
Book Design: Greg Tucker

Photo Credits: Cover, pp. 5, 7, 9, 13, 15, 17, 19, 21 Shutterstock.com; p. 11 © David McNew/Newsmakers/Getty Images.

Library of Congress Cataloging-in-Publication Data

Dayton, Connor.
  Volcanic rocks / Connor Dayton. — 1st ed.
      p. cm. — (Rocks and minerals)
  Includes index.
  ISBN-13: 978-1-4042-3688-2 (library binding)
  ISBN-10: 1-4042-3688-0 (library binding)
  1. Rocks, Igneous—Juvenile literature. 2. Volcanoes—Juvenile literature. I. Title.
  QE461.D349 2007
  552'.2—dc22
                                        2006030148

Manufactured in the United States of America

Contents

What Are Volcanic Rocks?

There are three types of rocks on Earth. They are **sedimentary rocks**, **metamorphic rocks**, and **igneous rocks**. Sedimentary rocks are formed when tiny pieces of matter build up and are pressed together. Over time this matter gets hard. Metamorphic rocks are formed when heat and **pressure** cause changes to sedimentary or igneous rocks. Igneous rocks are made when **molten** rock cools and hardens.

Volcanic rocks form when lava cools and hardens. Lava is molten rock that has **erupted** from a volcano. When molten rock is under Earth's **surface**, it is called magma.

These rocks on this beach in Hawaii are basalt.
Basalt is a rock formed when lava cools and hardens.

Volcanoes

Volcanoes are places where lava, gases, ash, and **pyroclastic debris** erupt from Earth's surface. Volcanoes are found all over the world, and they all have a few parts in common.

The place deep inside a volcano where the magma pools is called the magma chamber. The conduit is the pipe through which the magma flows toward the surface. The volcano's opening is called the crater. Dikes are smaller conduits that reach the surface. The opening at the end of a dike is a vent. A sill is made when the magma in a smaller conduit cools before it reaches the surface.

Inset diagram labels:
Ash and Rock
Crater
Vent
Sill
Dike
Conduit
Magma Chamber

Pyroclastic debris can build up on the sides of a volcano. Over time this makes the volcano bigger. *Inset:* This diagram shows the parts of a volcano.

Types of Lava

Lava is classified, or grouped, by its makeup. It is also grouped by how viscous it is, or how little it flows. The lava groupings are felsic, mafic, and intermediate. Different rocks form from the different types of lava.

Felsic lava is the most viscous and coolest lava. It has a lot of the mineral silica. Mafic lava is the least viscous and hottest lava. It has a lot of the minerals magnesium and iron. Intermediate lava flows more than felsic lava but less than mafic lava. Intermediate lava is not as cool as felsic lava but not as hot as mafic lava. It has a lot of magnesium and iron, too.

This is a flow of mafic lava. It is cooling into a bumpy sheet of basalt. Hawaiians call lava that flows and cools in this way *aa*.

Cooling Off

The way in which lava cools and hardens also plays a part in the kind of volcanic rock that forms. That means that each type of lava can make many different kinds of rocks. For example, obsidian, pumice, and rhyolite all form from felsic lava that has cooled in different ways.

When felsic lava cools quickly, it hardens into a glassy black rock called obsidian. If the lava gets filled with gas bubbles, it can form pumice. Pumice is full of holes and looks like a **sponge**. Solid, light-colored rhyolite forms when the lava cools slowly.

Rhyolite is only one of the types of rock that form from felsic lava. This rhyolite is near the Mammoth Lakes, in California.

Basalt

Basalt is the most common type of volcanic rock. It is formed from quickly cooled mafic lava. Basalt is dark and comes in colors from gray to black.

Basalt can come in different shapes and textures, or feels. How the lava erupted and where it flowed are what form different types of basalt. For example, pillows form when the lava erupts under the ocean and cools quickly. They form into rounded shapes that have glassy surfaces. Tiny pieces of basalt also make up the ash that is shot into the air in volcanic eruptions.

Basalt can take on many forms. Here the basalt has taken a shape called a column. Basalt columns can form when a thick flow of mafic lava cools quickly. The quick cooling can cause the rock to break into columns.

13

Obsidian

Another common type of volcanic rock is obsidian. It forms when felsic lava cools quickly. Obsidian is black and looks shiny. It is a type of natural glass.

People have used obsidian for many different things. It can be used as a gemstone. Long ago obsidian was shined to make **mirrors**. It also has been used to make **arrowheads**. In fact, obsidian can make such a sharp blade that today it is used to make cutting tools!

Obsidian has long been valued for its many uses as well as its beauty. This shiny black obsidian stands out from the landscape around it.

Pumice

Pumice is also a common volcanic rock. It can come in different colors, such as white, yellow, gray, brown, and red. Pumice forms when felsic lava erupts into the air and gets gas trapped in it. The gas leaves lots of holes in the rock. Sometimes this makes pumice so light that it can float in water.

People have used pumice to make a lightweight **concrete** for buildings. Another everyday use for pumice is to smooth things. Lots of people use pumice to smooth the bottoms of their feet!

Pumice is a lightweight volcanic rock. This piece has so many holes in it that it might float in water!

Other Volcanic Rocks

There are many other, less common types of volcanic rocks. A few of them are bombs, tuff, and Pele's hair.

Bombs are formed when globs of thick lava are thrown high into the air during an eruption. The lava cools as it falls and hardens into a rounded shape before it hits the ground. Tuff is rock made out of volcanic ash that has built up and been been pressed together. Pele's hair forms when lava is blown by the wind into thin strings. It is named for Hawaii's goddess of volcanoes.

These large pieces of tuff in Turkey have had caves cut into them.

Volcanic Islands

A volcano that is under the ocean can form an island. This happens over a long period of time during which volcanic eruptions cause a large buildup of rocks. Examples of volcanic islands are the Mariana Islands and the Aleutian Islands. These are in the Pacific Ocean.

One of the newest volcanic islands is Surtsey, which was formed in 1963. It is in the Atlantic Ocean, off the coast of Iceland. Iceland is the world's largest volcanic island.

Wizard Island is another volcanic island. It is in Crater Lake, in Oregon.

Always Changing

There are volcanoes all around the world that are active, or still erupting. This means that there are still volcanoes erupting lava, ash, and other pyroclastic debris. This means that new volcanic rocks are still being made. It also means that Earth's surface is always changing.

Once they are made, volcanic rocks do not always stay the same. Over time if there is enough heat and pressure, a volcanic rock can be changed into a metamorphic rock. This changing between types of rocks is known as the rock cycle.

Glossary

arrowheads (ER-oh-hedz) The sharp ends of hunting tools that are shot with a bow.

concrete (KON-kreet) A mix of water, stones, sand, and other things. Concrete becomes very hard and strong when it dries.

erupted (ih-RUP-ted) To have sent up gases, smoke, or lava.

igneous rocks (IG-nee-us ROKS) Hot, melted, underground minerals that have cooled and hardened.

metamorphic rocks (meh-tuh-MOR-fik ROKS) Rocks that have been changed by heat and heavy weight.

mirrors (MIR-urz) Flat surfaces that show what is placed in front of them.

molten (MOHL-ten) Melted by heat.

pressure (PREH-shur) A force that pushes on something.

pyroclastic debris (py-roh-KLAS-tik dih-BREE) The hot gases, ash, and rocks that come from a volcano.

sedimentary rocks (seh-deh-MEN-teh-ree ROKS) Stones, sand, or mud that has been pressed together to form rock.

sponge (SPUNJ) A holey tool used to clean things.

surface (SER-fes) The outside of anything.

Index

A

arrowheads, 14

C

concrete, 16

I

igneous rocks, 4

M

magma, 4, 6

metamorphic
  rock(s), 4, 22
mirrors, 14
molten rock, 4

P

pressure, 4, 22
pumice, 10, 16
pyroclastic
  debris, 6, 22

R

rhyolite, 10

S

sedimentary
  rocks, 4

V

volcano(es), 4, 6,
  18, 20, 22

Web Sites

Due to the changing nature of Internet links, PowerKids Press has developed an online list of Web sites related to the subject of this book. This site is updated regularly. Please use this link to access the list:
www.powerkidslinks.com/romi/vorock/

24